Hello, Family Members,

Learning to read is one of the most important accomp~~.~~ of early childhood. **Hello Reader!** books are designed to help children become skilled readers who like to read. Beginning readers learn to read by remembering frequently used words like "the," "is," and "and"; by using phonics skills to decode new words; and by interpreting picture and text clues. These books provide both the stories children enjoy and the structure they need to read fluently and independently. Here are suggestions for helping your child *before*, *during*, and *after* reading:

Before

- Look at the cover and pictures and have your child predict what the story is about.
- Read the story to your child.
- Encourage your child to chime in with familiar words and phrases.
- Echo read with your child by reading a line first and having your child read it after you do.

During

- Have your child think about a word he or she does not recognize right away. Provide hints such as "Let's see if we know the sounds" and "Have we read other words like this one?"
- Encourage your child to use phonics skills to sound out new words.
- Provide the word for your child when more assistance is needed so that he or she does not struggle and the experience of reading with you is a positive one.
- Encourage your child to have fun by reading with a lot of expression . . . like an actor!

After

- Have your child keep lists of interesting and favorite words.
- Encourage your child to read the books over and over again. Have him or her read to brothers, sisters, grandparents, and even teddy bears. Repeated readings develop confidence in young readers.
- Talk about the stories. Ask and answer questions. Share ideas about the funniest and most interesting characters and events in the stories.

I do hope that you and your child enjoy this book.

—Francie Alexander
Reading Specialist,
Scholastic's Instructional Publishing Group

To Pam and Leo Kinsella,
the best parents in the world, and to my husband Bruce.
Thank you all for your support.

—A.B.

To Edie, with thanks

—P.G.

Text copyright © 1998 by Andrea Buckless.
Illustrations copyright © 1998 by Patti Goodnow.
All rights reserved. Published by Scholastic Inc.
SCHOLASTIC, HELLO READER! and CARTWHEEL BOOKS and associated logos are trademarks and/or registered trademarks of Scholastic Inc.

Library of Congress Cataloging-in-Publication Data
Buckless, Andrea.
    Class picture day / by Andrea Buckless; illustrated by Patti Goodnow.
    p. cm. — (Hello reader! Level 2)
"Cartwheel books."
Summary: The only student to stick her tongue out in the class picture has to figure out how to fix this terrible mistake.
ISBN 0-590-37975-5
    [1. Photographs—Fiction. 2. Schools—Fiction.] I. Goodnow, Patti, ill.
II. Title. III. Series.
PZ7.B8817C1 1998
[E]—dc21
                                                                98-18725
                                                                CIP
                                                                AC

10 9 8 7 6 5 4 3 2 1   8 9/9 0/0 01 02 03

Printed in the U.S.A.   24
First printing, December 1998

Class
–Picture–
Day

by Andrea Buckless
Illustrated by Patti Goodnow

Hello Reader! — Level 2

SCHOLASTIC INC.
Cartwheel ·B·O·O·K·S·®

New York   Toronto   London   Auckland   Sydney

"When the photographer says 'Cheese!'
stick out your tongue," said Amy.
"Okay," said Richard.
"Okay," I said.

The pictures came back.

Amy is smiling.

Richard is smiling.

My whole class is smiling!

I am sticking out my tongue.

Amy put her picture in her folder.
Richard put his picture in his bookbag.
I put my picture in the trash.

Just as I was leaving,
my teacher said,
"Don't forget your picture!"

We got on the bus.
Amy showed her picture to
the bus driver.

Richard showed his picture to
the big kids.
I stuck my picture
between the seats.

Just as I was leaving,
my bus driver said,
"Don't forget your picture!"

When we got off the bus,
Amy ran home with her picture.

Richard ran home with his picture.

I put my picture in my dog's house.

Just as I was leaving,
my dog ran up to me.
He had my picture in his mouth.

I had to take my picture home.

So I took out my red marker...

Now, Amy is sticking out her tongue.
Richard is sticking out his tongue.
My teacher is sticking out her tongue.
My whole class is sticking out their tongues!

I think I'll frame this picture!